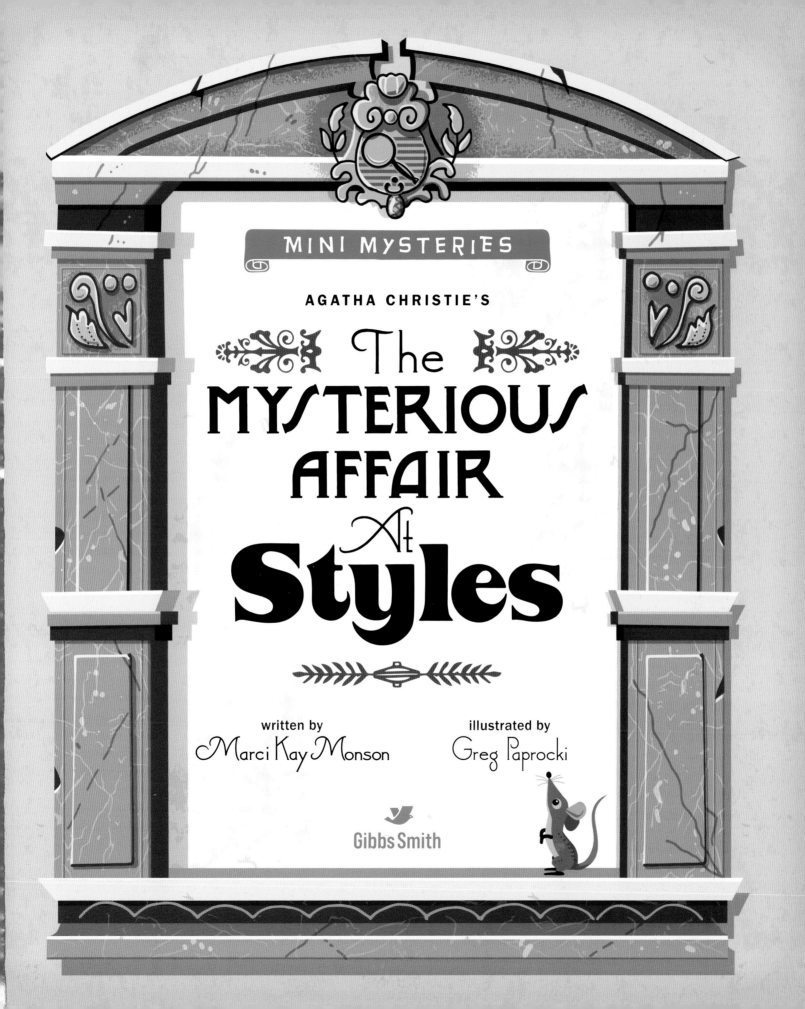

MINI MYSTERIES

AGATHA CHRISTIE'S

# The MYSTERIOUS AFFAIR At Styles

written by
Marci Kay Monson

illustrated by
Greg Paprocki

Gibbs Smith

EMILY
CAVENDISH
—
*A wealthy woman of
a certain age, widowed
and remarried*

ALFRED
INGLETHORPE
—
*Emily's spoiled
second husband,
a man of leisure*

HERCULE
POIROT
—
*Renowned
private detective*

EVELYN
HOWARD
—
*Emily's companion
and friend*

DORCUS
—
*Emily's
loyal maid*

## JOHN CAVENDISH

*Emily's eldest stepson from her late first husband's previous marriage, a lawyer*

## LAWRENCE CAVENDISH

*Emily's youngest stepson from her late first husband's previous marriage, a doctor*

## HASTINGS

*Poirot's shy rodent friend*

**Can you spot Hastings hiding in every spread of this book?**

## MARY CAVENDISH

*John's wife*

## CYNTHIA MURDOCH

*An orphaned family friend, a pharmacy worker*

# Enchanté, detectives!

I am Hercule Poirot, you know.
I'm sure you've heard my name.
Or at least you've heard of my moustache!
Solving mysteries is my game.

I am a famous detective.
I travel the world solving crimes.
People think I'm especially smart,
I've been told so plenty of times.

*Mon ami*, I need your help today!
I have a new case in the files.
Won't you come and help me solve

## — The — MYSTERIOUS AFFAIR At Styles?

There once was a family named Cavendish
who lived in a house named *Styles*.
A quiet home in a small English town,
the family was all smiles.

# Until...

Mr. Cavendish died and left Emily,
and his sons, Lawrence and John.
Years later, Emily met Alfred.
*Alas*, the three men did not get along.

Some thought Alfred was greedy,
including Evelyn, Emily's friend.
But Emily thought he was perfect,
and Evelyn left in the end.

## ACTIVITY

Can you match each family member
to the emotion they are feeling?
Draw a line with your finger from
one column to the other.

| | |
|---|---|
| JOHN | IN LOVE |
| CYNTHIA | PROUD |
| DORCAS | THOUGHTFUL |
| ALFRED | SAD |
| EMILY | ANGRY |
| HASTINGS | WORRIED |
| EVELYN | HAPPY |
| MARY | TIRED |
| LAWRENCE | SILLY |

JOHN

EMILY

CYNTHIA

DORCAS

ALFRED

HASTINGS

MARY

LAWRENCE

Early one morning, John woke up
to find that Emily was sick.
The doors to her room were all locked,
so getting inside was a trick.

But there was no hope for poor Emily.
When they broke in, she was gone.
She died in her beautiful bedroom,
just as the night turned to dawn.

And yet something didn't feel right.
The scene was not adding up.
What if Emily was not really sick?
Was a *poison* of sorts in her cup?

## ACTIVITY

Can you find these clues in the room?

**TEACUP**
**PURPLE BRIEFCASE**
**CARPET STAIN**
**DARK GREEN FABRIC**
**CANDLE WAX DRIPPINGS**
**CRUMPLED PAPER**

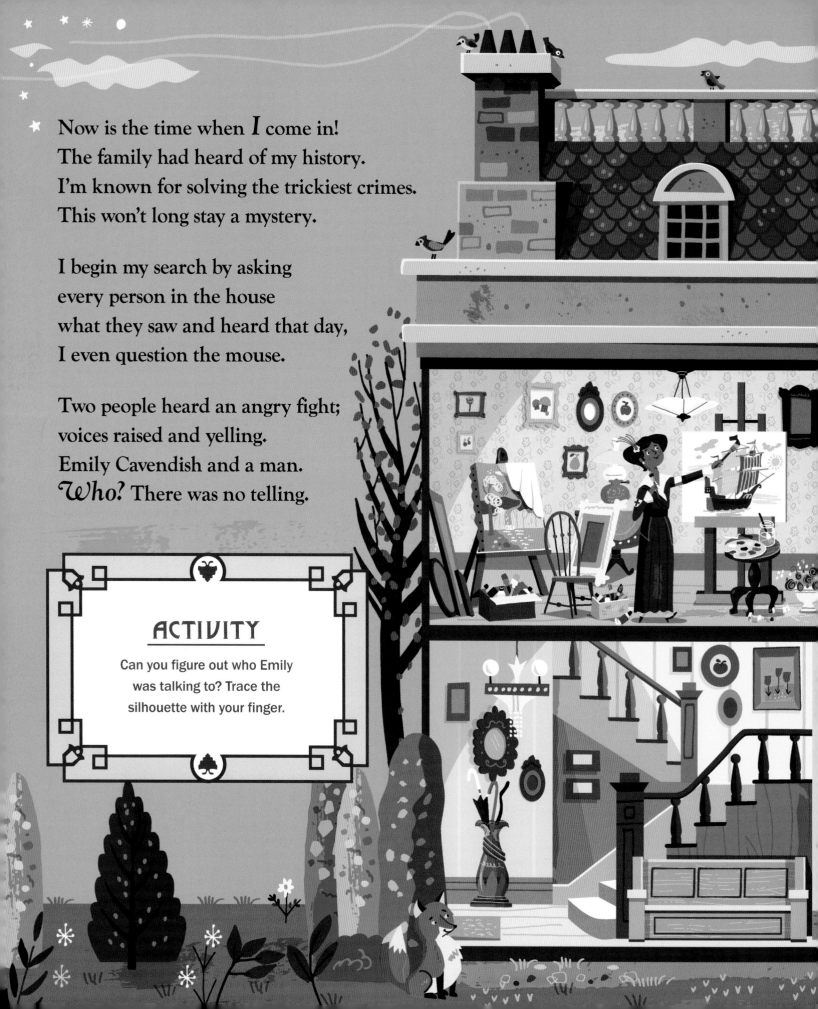

Now is the time when *I* come in!
The family had heard of my history.
I'm known for solving the trickiest crimes.
This won't long stay a mystery.

I begin my search by asking
every person in the house
what they saw and heard that day,
I even question the mouse.

Two people heard an angry fight;
voices raised and yelling.
Emily Cavendish and a man.
*Who?* There was no telling.

## ACTIVITY

Can you figure out who Emily
was talking to? Trace the
silhouette with your finger.

As I talk to each witness at hand,
I start gathering clues.
I even question Evelyn.
Who came back when she heard the news.

Footprints outside the window.
A piece of fabric, dark green.
Could someone have come into her room?
Then slipped outside unseen?

Everyone thinks it is Alfred.
They believe he's a very bad man.
But he wasn't home when it happened,
Unless *he* was the one who ran?

## ACTIVITY

Using your finger, help Poirot get
back to town through the maze.

It seems they *all* have a reason.
*Each* could have committed the crime.
Evelyn is a nurse, and mad at her friend,
but she wasn't there at the time.

John really needs the money
he should have received from his dad.
Mary doesn't even like her family,
she always seems so sad.

Lawrence was meant for a doctor.
Now he writes poems that aren't good.
Cynthia works in a pharmacy.
Poison someone, she could!

## ACTIVITY

Can you find these reminders of clues
in the picture frames?

**FOOTPRINTS**
**TEACUP**
**QUILL PEN**
**MONEY**
**EYEGLASSES**
**A MEDICAL CROSS**
**POISON BOTTLE**

Soon the case is brought to court
Where judge and jury hear facts.
They ask many questions, hear all the sides.
Do they find any clues I lack?

It is time to bring in the experts.
(Though truly, *I'm* expert enough!)
A doctor agrees it *is* poison, but
isn't sure how she took the stuff.

The pharmacist says he saw Alfred
out buying poison one night.
He even has his signature,
Though the handwriting isn't quite right.

## ACTIVITY

Can you find the poison bottle?

### HINT
It has this symbol on it: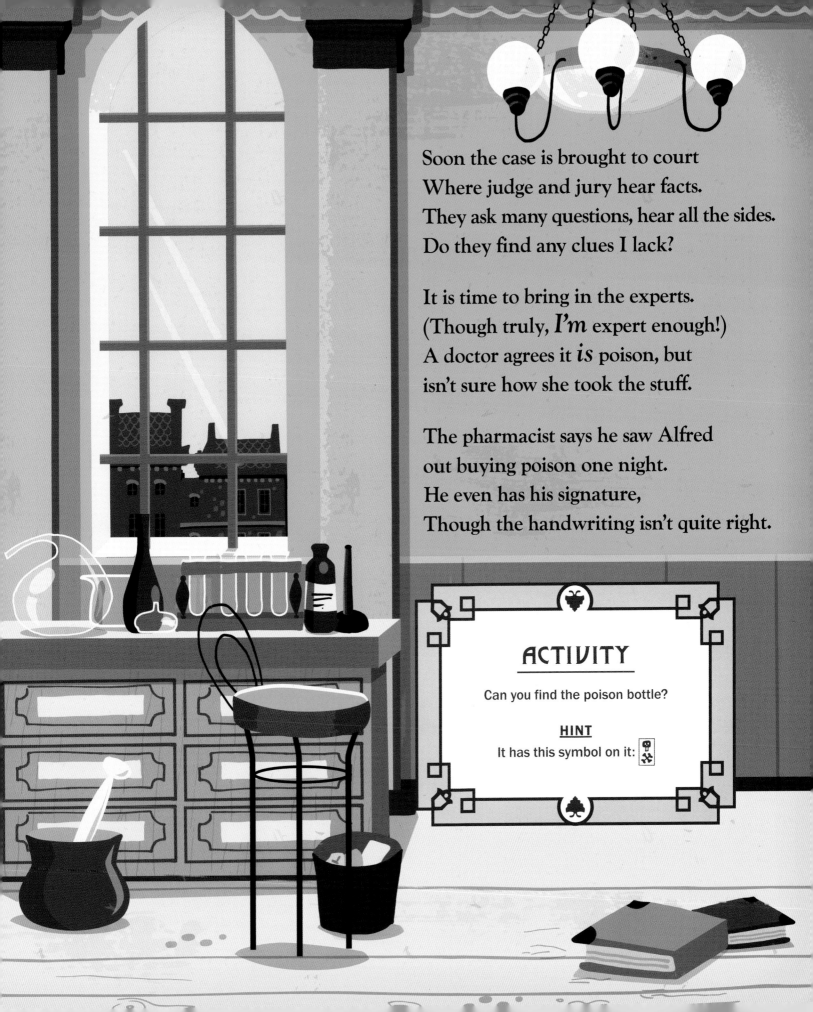

The judge agrees with the family
and thinks Alfred's caught red-handed.
There still isn't very much evidence
but "Arrest him!" they've all demanded.

I leave the court feeling puzzled.
Something isn't quite right.
It seems Alfred *wanted* to be caught.
He hardly put up a fight!

Perhaps he knows, as I do,
that if they take him without proof
he'll be let go, free as a bird,
and the whole case will go *poof.*

## ACTIVITY

Pretend you're the judge. Would
you arrest Alfred? Don't forget to
bang the gavel!

I tell the police what I've noticed.
They agree not to catch him today.
I go back to Styles, thinking hard,
And run right into Dorcas, the maid!

"I just remembered—in the attic!
There are dress-ups in an old chest.
Maybe something there could help you?
I think there was a green dress."

*Mais oui!* The green thread
from the crime scene!
I race to the room to find out.
But no, the dress is not quite right,
Though what I *do* find makes me shout!

(Do *you* see the clue I found?)

## ACTIVITY

Starting in the top right corner,
follow the green thread with your
finger to find the dress!

There, in the corner of the attic:
the perfect Alfred disguise!
A fake beard—gigantic and black—
and thick glasses to hide the eyes.

Alfred did not buy the poison.
A person in costume, I think.
The pieces seem to be falling in place,
but I just can't quite find the link.

The police next arrest John Cavendish,
but they have no evidence, you see!
You really *must* have plenty of proof,
so eventually John is freed.

## ACTIVITY

Can you spot the differences
between these two people?
Which one is the real Alfred?

In Emily's room, I find a box.
It opens with a special key.
In the box is a crumpled-up letter.
I carefully start to read:

"Dearest Evelyn, do not worry!
The poisoning will happen tonight.
Your plan to put it in her medicine
was *genius*! It will work out all right . . ."

The letter is torn at the bottom,
but I'd know the writing anywhere.
It is time to call in the family
to uncover the deadly affair.

## ACTIVITY

Can you find which key opens the case?
Who committed the crime?

"Let me introduce you to the murderers!
Alfred Inglethorpe and Evelyn Howard!"
They try to escape from the back of the room,
but they soon find themselves overpowered.

You see, my friends, they had fallen in love,
and sometimes love is funny.
Evelyn just *pretended* to hate Alfred,
But it all came down to the money.

When Emily Cavendish died that night,
she'd left Alfred her money, her land.
He schemed and he planned to be with
Evelyn, to have a life so grand!

## ACTIVITY

Did you guess the right person?
Make sure to yell: "J'accuse!"

But it wasn't to be for those lovebirds.
Hercule Poirot to the rescue again!
We caught them both in their evil plot.
Thank you, detectives—my friends!

We used our little gray brain cells.
Relied on order, and method, and facts.
*Voilà! Très bien! Merci, mon ami,*
another case has been cracked.

As for the Cavendish family,
that was the end of their trials.
And this is the story of how we solved
The MYSTERIOUS AFFAIR
At **Styles.**

Congratulations,
detectives!

You have
solved the case.

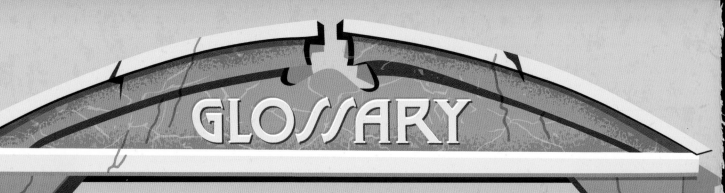

# GLOSSARY

*Ah non!*
French for "Oh no!"

**Affair**
an event or a performance

**Arrested/Arresting**
seize (someone) by legal authority and take into custody

**Court**
a place where justice is administered

**Crime**
an action or an instance of negligence that is legally prohibited

**Disguise**
to change the appearance of oneself so as to conceal identity or mislead

*Enchanté*
French for "nice to meet you"

**Evidence**
that which tends to prove or disprove something

*J'accuse!*
French for "I accuse you!"

**Judge**
a public officer authorized to hear and decide cases in a court of law

**Jury**
a group of persons sworn to render a verdict

*Mais oui!*
French for "But yes!"

# GLOSSARY

**Merci**
French for "thank you"

**Mon ami**
French for "my friend"

**Mystery**
something that is impossible or difficult to understand or explain

**Pharmacy**
a place where you buy medicine

**Poison**
a substance with an inherent property that tends to
destroy life or impair health

**Red-handed**
in the very act of a crime, wrongdoing, etc.

**Signature**
a person's name, or a mark representing it, as signed personally

**Très bien**
French for "very good"

**Voilà!**
French for "There it is!"

❁

**Pronunciation Guide**
Hercule Poirot
*(Hur-kyool Pwaa-row)*

FIRST EDITION
28 27 26 25 24    5 4 3 2 1

Text © 2024 Marci Kay Monson
Illustrations © 2024 Greg Paprocki

This children's book is based on Agatha Christie's
*The Mysterious Affair at Styles*.

Published by
Gibbs Smith
570 N. Sportsplex Dr.
Kaysville, UT 84037

1.800.835.4993 orders
www.gibbs-smith.com

Designed by Greg Paprocki and Ryan Thomann
Manufactured in Guangdong, China, in June 2024 by SkyDragon Printing

Library of Congress Control Number: 2023951454
ISBN: 978-1-4236-6756-8

This product is made of FSC®-certified and other controlled material.

MIX
Paper from
responsible sources
FSC® C081635